Hidden Secrets

Tabitha Kremesec

DORRANCE PUBLISHING CO
EST. 1920
PITTSBURGH, PENNSYLVANIA 15238

Dorrance Publishing Co
585 Alpha Drive
Pittsburgh, PA 15238
Visit our website at *www.dorrancebookstore.com*

ISBN: 979-8-89341-040-2
eISBN: 979-8-89341-539-1

Hidden Secrets

*D*ear diary, my family has a dark secret. Let me first start by introducing myself. my name is Lynn Robbins; I have brown hair and blue eyes, am petite, and have a good sense of humor. I'm an honest person, but I may be too honest. I express thoughts and feelings without considering the effect it might have on others. I'm really sensitive and able to pick up on the feelings of others, and I love being a nurturer.

I'm sixteen and live with my parents and three brothers. My mom's name is Lily. She has blonde hair and is chubby. She's not easy to talk to; she gets angry quickly. Lily is always irritable; she thinks she's God's gift to the world. Lily feels since she has money, she owns everyone. My dad's name is Fred; he is tall and skinny. Fred is angry at the world; he thinks he's smarter than anyone. He's lazy, has a short fuse, and has a bleak personality. My three brothers are short and round. My brother's name is Rick; he is selfish and dislikes sharing anything. He never shows up to events when he says he's going to, and he doesn't like to be rushed. Jimmy is quiet and does not like conflict. He dislikes talking, and his communication skills are almost nonexistent. Tony, he is funny and what a character. He's like me in ways; he's a smooth talker, kind and loving, and he would give his shirt off his back if you needed one. My brothers are in middle school. They are triplets.

We live in El Dorado Hills; we are wealthy and have a big house. The house is made of red brick and is a two-story house. When you walk into the house, the floors are marble. It is a beautiful home with many secrets. My dad is a lawyer, and my mom is a homemaker. My family has a dark secret. I wouldn't say I like to talk about it, but it has to be said. My dad, Fred, uses cocaine, and when he uses it, Fred beats my brothers. While this is happening, my mom gets drunk.

My parents don't know this, but I called the police and reported their abuse, trying to help my brothers in any way I could. As I write this, I hear a knock at the door; it's my mom, Lily. As my mom had me go down to the living room, she growled that the police were in the kitchen and they wanted to talk to me. The police said facetiously that they didn't believe me about the abuse and drug use; my mom and dad were unhappy with me and decided to kick me out of the house.

I'm scared. I have nowhere to go; they gave me some cash and my car. It was late, so I packed my belongings and said goodbye to my brothers. As I drove down the driveway, I could see my brothers crying. What have I done? I was only trying to help them. I had an idea of where to go; I would go up north to my grandma's.

As I traveled the highway, I thought of ways to help my brothers. I soon arrived at my grandma's small white house, which only had two bedrooms. Not what I was used to, but it was a roof over my head. It was morning by this time. I knocked on the door, and my grandma answered; her name was Betty. She is a lovely lady, very nurturing, and always has good things to say about people. Sometimes, she can be a smarty-pants. Betty is tall and thin. She likes to lie about everything; she finds it entertaining to tell lies about events that never happened to make her life seem more interesting. Betty is my dad's mom.

Betty said very amiably that I could live here for a while.

When I came into the house, I went straight to the kitchen. The room was small, and there was a tiny table with some flowers in the center. I went over and smelled the carnations. As I looked around, I could tell that my grandma hadn't cleaned in a while. The white curtains were stained from the cooking grease, and the white walls had turned yellow.

My grandma asked eagerly if I was hungry. I told her I was, and that cereal sounded good. I told her everything that happened last night at my parents' house. Betty was shocked to hear that her son does drugs and beats my brothers. My grandma said, in a bossy manner, that I have to start school at Northern High first thing tomorrow.

As I settled into my new room, the phone rang. I heard Betty yelling, and then it went silent. I didn't think anything of it, so I just started watching TV, but my curiosity got the best of me. I heard the phone ring again, so I ran to the phone and answered it. It was my mom. She started yelling and screaming at me, so I just hung up. I tried to fight back the tears but wasn't able to. I just started bawling, and my mom hurt my feelings once again.

I went into the living room and saw my grandma crying. So, I sat down and asked her quietly what was wrong. She said with pain in her voice my dad, Fred, had disowned her. All this is happening because of me. I hugged my Grandma Betty and told her everything would be alright.

The day flew by fast. I was getting tired and had a big day tomorrow; I'd be starting a new school and making new friends. Morning came quickly. I was still tired, but I knew I had to go to school. I drove myself to school and thought the whole way about how I would save my brothers.

My day at school went well; I met a couple of friends. We're going out to the movies later tonight. It's only Monday, and I already wish it was Friday; I had such a busy day today at school. I'm looking forward to going to the movies tonight with Nancy Mabon. She is a downer, a little silly, likes to fight, and can be bossy. I do enjoy Nancy's sense of humor. For that reason alone, I like hanging out with her. Nancy is my new friend; she has red hair and lots of freckles on her face.

Jack Fletcher, the other person I'm going to the movies with, has black hair and green eyes. Jack is an oddball, has the strangest personality, is brilliant, and pretends to be overly friendly, but he likes to talk smack about others. Unfortunately, Jack, Nancy's boyfriend, hangs out with us.

I'm back from the movies now. My grandma Betty was asleep when I came home, so I went straight to my room. Nancy and Jack were so open with their life tonight that I found out Nancy was adopted, and Jack's dad died in the war.

I woke up this morning and thought I would see a lawyer. I went to the kitchen and talked with my grandma, Betty. She asked, shocked, what I was doing going to a lawyer. I told her I wanted to try to get my brothers so they could live here with me.

My grandma said sternly that only I could live with her; she didn't have room for my brothers.

I decided to go to the lawyers anyway. As I drove down the highway, a thought came to me: if I were to drop out of school and get a full-time job, I might just be able to get my brothers. I arrived at the lawyer's office. The lawyer's name was Ken, and Ken's appearance reminded me of my dad. His attitude also reminded me of my dad; it must be a lawyer's attitude. That was a short meeting, and I discovered that if I get emancipated and have a full-time job, I might have an excellent chance to get my brothers. Ken also said bluntly that I need to find a place to live that's big enough for my brothers, a full-time job, and a GED.

I went home to my Grandma Betty and told her my plan. Betty thought it was good. Suddenly, the phone rang, and my grandma answered it.

Betty said with concern, "It's your brother, Rick. He sounds terrified."

I ran to the phone and asked what was wrong. Rick was crying, he asked eagerly when I was coming home. I told him I couldn't come home; Rick then told me something disturbing and when I heard it, I just fell to the floor crying. Rick, Jimmy, and Tony are being beaten worse than before, Rick said sadly. They're not getting fed anymore; they're having to sneak food. I had to do something soon.

The following day, I woke up with the worst headache; my nose was stuffy, and my eyes were swollen. I went to the kitchen and told my Grandma Betty I was looking for a job today. Betty happily said there was a job opening at the grocery store.

As I started out the door, the phone rang so I answered it, it was my brother, Tony. He was so upset. I asked, worried, what was wrong. He was crying so much that I couldn't understand him. I tried to get him to calm down, and after about ten minutes, he finally calmed down. Tony finally was able to speak and said furiously that ur dad, Fred, was so angry with Rick last night that Fred gave Rick a concussion. Rick is in the hospital in a coma. I asked Tony how Dad gave Rick a concussion. Tony said, frustrated, that dad threw him down the stairs outside, and Rick hit his head on the concrete. I asked loudly if the cops were involved.

Tony said coldly, "Our dad said to the police it was an accident."

I was crying by this time and I told my brother, "Tony, I'm trying to find a way for you guys to come live with me."

Tony was so excited to hear this. I told Tony that I was on my way to get a job right now and to keep me informed on Rick's condition.

As I hung up the phone, I told my Grandma Betty what Tony had told me.

My grandma just stood there with a stunned look on her face. Betty then started crying and said, "Lynn, I'm so sorry that your dad is so abusive. I wish that everything was different and your dad was a more likable man. I don't know where I went wrong raising your father; I feel like I own this."

I replied, "Why, Grandma?"

Betty then answered in a quivering tone, "I used to smack your father around."

I hugged my grandma and said, "I love you, but I must go. I have an interview today."

The interview went well. The lady who interviewed me was named Kim. She had black hair and was slender; she had a goofy sense of humor, and she was dressed in a cowgirl dress. Kim said excitedly that I had a good chance of getting the job and she would call me in a few days.

As I drove down the highway, many thoughts ran through my head. I was thinking of seeing Nancy and Jack. I needed someone to talk to besides my Grandma Betty. I went to Nancy's house first; her house was like a little cottage tucked away in the forest. Luckily, she was home. As I walked up to the front door, I was just about ready to knock when a hand touched my shoulder. I jumped, frightened, and spun around to find Jack staring at me with the biggest grin. We exchanged words for a while, talking about different movies and the latest new music hits, until Nancy opened the door. Nancy, Jack, and I had fun. We talked all day. They gave me some ideas on how to get my brothers, but the ideas were silly. Nancy said jokingly that I should just kidnap them, and Jack said thoughtfully that I should just kill my parents. Both ideas won't work; I must keep to my plan: get a job, be emancipated, and get a GED.

A couple of days passed, and Kim still had no word on whether or not I was getting the job. I decided to go to the kitchen and get something to eat. My Grandma Betty stood in my doorway. I asked considerately what she wanted. Betty said calmly that Kim from the grocery store was on the phone. I ran to the phone. I was so excited to hear if I got the job.

Kim sounded disappointed when she talked; she said she was sorry to tell me I didn't get the job. Kim explained that the job is more than thirty hours each week. "I feel like this job will hurt your academic achievement."

I was in disbelief. I was sure I was going to get the job. What am I going to do now? I'm never going to get my brothers.

Just as I hung up the phone, the phone rang again. I answered it, and it was my brother Tony. I asked him curiously how Rick was doing.

Tony said sadly, "Rick is still in a coma, but his condition is improving. The doctors are hopeful." Tony said, disappointed, "Dad's not even visiting Rick in the hospital."

I told Tony that I'm coming to visit and that I don't care what our parents say or think. I hung up the phone.

I told my Grandma Betty that I was going to visit Rick in the hospital. I went to my room, started packing, and said goodbye to my grandma.

As I drove back to El Dorado Hills, thoughts were racing through my head. It is a three-hour drive from my grandma's to El Dorado Hills, so I had a lot of time to think.

I pulled into the memorial hospital. Luckily, I found a parking space nearby. I went to the front desk and found out what room my brother Rick was in. As I walked into the room, my brothers, Jimmy and Tony, and our mom, Lily, were sitting by my brother Rick's bedside. Instantly, Tony and Jimmy came running up to me and hugged me. My mom, Lily, just sat there and stared in disbelief. I went over and hugged my mom. Surprisingly, she hugged me back. She told me that she loved me and missed me.

My mom, Lily, said with concern in her voice that she wanted to talk to me alone in the chapel. As we walked down the long hallway, we finally reached the elevator. As we entered the elevator, it was filled with patients; it looked like there was no more room for two more people. My mom, Lily, and I finally reached the chapel; it was completely empty. There was no one in sight.

My mom, Lily, started to cry. She was shaking so badly that I thought she was having a seizure.

Confused, I asked why she wanted to talk to me alone. She said shakily she has a dark secret, and it's time to come out. I was all ears and curious. I had a feeling it wasn't good. As Lily tried to speak, she mumbled and stuttered, making it hard to determine what she was saying. I finally understood what she was saying and had to have her repeat it. My mom, Lily, told me that my brothers are not my full brothers.

Lily began telling me the story of her past. She said Rick, Jimmy, and Tony are not my dad Fred's kids. But actually, my dad Fred's brother Rob's kids, I was in disbelief when I heard this. Lily said sadly that Rob died in a car accident shortly after the affair. That's why my dad Fred abuses my brothers. Fred is so angry with his brother Rob that he takes it out on my brothers because Rob's dead.

My mom, Lily, started crying uncontrollably. I comforted her as well as I could under the circumstances. I was sad for my mom, and I felt ashamed that my mom would cheat on my dad. I told my mom that she needed to leave Fred. Lily said she was terrified of leaving Fred. I asked, wondering why my mom, Lily, was so scared. She said, terrified, that Fred threatened to kill her if she ever left him. My mom, Lily, and I talked briefly. I told her my plans to save my brothers. My mom, Lily, actually likes the idea.

We started back to Rick's room. To our surprise, Rick had woken up from his coma. Mom and I ran over to his bedside and started kissing and hugging him. Rick was so excited to see me. We had so much catching up to do, but the doctor said he needed rest, and visiting hours were over. I told Rick and Jimmy of my plans to get them.

Tony was standing by my side, and he said bravely to me. "I was going to tell our brothers about your plan to rescue us when the time was right when Mom and Dad weren't around."

I looked at Mom and told her she needed to tell them the truth about my dad, Fred. Lily spoke with such concern in her voice that she said when the time is right, and now is not the time. I decided to drive home tonight instead of staying in El Dorado Hills for a couple of days.

As I drove home, I thought about what my mom said about my brother's father. I started thinking of how I could get my father, Fred, out of the picture. I love my brothers so much that I didn't care if they were my half-brothers. I do love my mom, even though she was unfaithful to my dad. And I have mixed emotions when it comes to caring for my dad.

It's early Saturday morning. I woke up and am startedto look for a job. I'm so eager to get a job. I started looking through the wanted ads; you must have a high school diploma or GED in every job I seem to come across. I was beginning to get discouraged, and then I saw a small ad on the back of the paper. As I read it, it said dog walking; this excited me. I thought to myself, 'I could do this. How hard can this be?' There was a phone number, so I decided to call it.

A lady answered. She sounded very snooty. She gave an interview over the phone. The chat went well. I discovered her name is Shauna Myers, and she owns the business. She was unfriendly, very touchy, easily offended, and irritated. Shauna said, annoyed, that I could start today. I asked curiously how many hours were available and what the pay was.

Shauna said rudely, "It's eight hours a day, seven days a week, and pays $20 an hour."

I hung up the phone, dressed and then entered the kitchen. My Grandma Betty was making breakfast. She was frying eggs, and I could smell the bacon cooking. I told my grandma that I have a job dog walking.

My grandma said with excitement, "That's wonderful. When do you start?"

I replied happily, "I start today. I had my interview over the phone this morning."

I hurried and ate my breakfast. The eggs were raw, and the bacon was overcooked, but all was good. My Grandma Betty doesn't know how to cook but always makes an effort.

As I walked out the door to my car, I heard my grandma yelling.

"Have a good day at work," she said, overly happy.

As I drove down the highway, I was taken in by the scenery. My mind was clear this time, and I never noticed the beauty of my surroundings. The oak trees had almost lost all their leaves, but the trees that still had leaves were a pretty yellow. There were many trees, such as pine, cedar, and cottonwood. This little town of Willows is the perfect place to have a family; its population is about six thousand.

I pulled up to Shauna's office building and noticed the big yard with old fencing. The office had just opened, and many dogs were waiting to be walked. There were a few different breeds, such as German shepherds, bulldogs, and labrador retrievers. The dogs are jumping around and barking, feeling the stress of shelter life.

As I walked through the office door, Shauna was there and greeted me. Shauna was of medium build and had red hair and glasses. She looked to be in her fifties.

Shauna said happily, "It's good to meet you in person, and good morning. I have someone that I want to introduce you to."

As I waited for her to return, I thought to myself, 'Shauna is different in person than over the phone, but she still seems a little stuck up, very proud, and conceited.'

Shauna returned shortly with a man. He was so dreamy my knees were buckling, and I was at a loss for words. He was built and muscular, about 5'5". He had the most beautiful eyes. They were green like emeralds; his hair was sand-colored, and when he spoke, it sent chills up my spine.

Shauna asked quietly if I was okay.

I shook my head, "Yes, I'm fine."

Shauna introduced me, and she said "nicely" sarcastically. "This is Shane. He will be working with you walking dogs alongside you." Shauna said quickly, "You kids better get started with walking these dogs."

Shane and I agreed, and we started off.

I was so nervous and shy as Shane and I took the dogs for a walk.

Shane started the conversation by asking me how old I was, where I lived and went to school, and about my family.

I didn't want to go into it with him, but he was trying to get to know me. I opened up. I told him the whole story of my life. I told him about my brothers being beaten and starved. I told him of my plans to get my brothers.

Shane was intrigued. I didn't feel so awkward around him anymore. He made me feel at ease; I was determined to learn about Shane and his life, so I asked questions. I asked all the questions that he asked me. Shane was frisky and sounded pleased that I showed interest in him.

Shane said he was overjoyed that he was twenty-one and lived two miles away in town. Shane said he was very disappointed that he's an only child and lives with his mom. His mom's name is Judy. She has MS and is bound to a wheelchair because all of her muscles have deteriorated. Shane said, dissatisfied that he wishes he could do more for his mom. I began to ask him about his dad, and Shane became very irritated. He became very hostile with his words. I told him he didn't have to talk about it right now or at all. Shane then began to calm down.

Shane and I headed back to the office with the dogs in hand. Shauna was there waiting for us to return so she could close up the building. She had a curious personality, but she's been unpleasant and somewhat aggressive with me.

I was glad the day was over and I could return home. As I arrived home to my Grandma Betty's house, I found a car parked in the driveway. I didn't recognize the ca. rI wondered who was there.

I was very nosy when I came into the house. "Hi Grandma, who's here?" I said with a lot of curiosity.

As I entered the house, I saw my Grandma Betty on the floor, passed out, and a man hovering over her. I was scared; I was frightened. I didn't know what was going on; all I knew was there was this man over my grandma on the floor, trying to revive her.

I ran over there to my Grandma Betty, who was lying on the floor.

I asked the man, "Who are you? What are you doing here? What have you done to my Grandma?"

I asked the man to call 911. He said it was already done and the ambulance should be on its way.

I was so confused; I didn't understand who this man was. I had never seen him before that I could recall. Just as I was ready to ask the man his name and explain what he was doing at my grandma's house, the ambulance showed up.

By this time, I was gathering my stuff and headed toward the hospital right behind the ambulance. The man asked if he could come with me, so I decided I would let him take a ride with me so he could explain himself.

The man decided that it was time for him to tell me why he was at my grandma's house. I was all ears, of course, and very curious and very worried at the same time. The man decided to disclose everything to me, and when he did, I was in utter shock. I found out that this man was my dad's brother, Rob.

When he disclosed who he was, the only thing I could do was question, "Where have you been all this time? I thought you died in the accident. What's going on?"

Rob looked at me. He said, "Listen, calm down. Let me explain. I had to fake my death. My brother was trying to kill me. I was scared. I had no choice in the matter. Nobody in the family knew I was faking my death."

I just got so confused that I started yelling out, "Why now? Do you have any idea what this has done to our family with you pretending to be dead? We were so depressed and sad. We thought we lost you for good. Not to mention what my brothers have been going through with my dad abusing them. My dad blames you and Mom for their birth and for cheating on him."

Rob looked down to his feet and started crying. He said he was so sorry that he wanted to compensate for the lost time.

I begin to tell Rob everything. Everything that's been going on and being kicked out of the house, trying to save my brothers. Then all of a sudden, I got this idea: I don't need to get emancipated. I don't need to get a house of my own. All my answers are right here: my Uncle Rob can get my brothers back and get custody of them because he's their dad. Just as I finished this thought, I noticed we were at the hospital already.

The EMTs were getting my grandma out of the ambulance and rushing her into the emergency room. I ran after them, and they told us to wait for the doctor. In the meantime, time was going by so slowly, and I was talking with my Uncle Rob. We were discussing how we were going to save my brothers, how we were going to reveal that he was still alive to the rest of the family, and how to introduce him to my brothers, who had never met him.

The doctor finally came out and talked to me and said that my grandma had a heart attack and she's in recovery now. They didn't know what the damage was just yet, if any. The doctor said that she was resting right now and it would be better to come back tomorrow. So with that being said, I decided that I would go home and talk with Uncle Rob.

Early the next morning, I was off to see my grandma at the hospital. As I drove down, I was by myself. I was feeling sad and feeling guilty that I couldn't do more for my grandma. All kinds of thoughts came rushing into my head. I was so confused I didn't know where to start.

I didn't know how to talk to my grandma about Uncle Rob. As I entered the hospital room that my grandma was recovering in, she saw me and started to cry. She said she dreamed that her son Rob was still alive. I sat down beside her. I began to cry, and I took her hands in mine; I then began to tell her she wasn't dreaming, that Rob was alive. My Grandma Betty was relieved to find out her son Rob was alive.

A few weeks went by, and my grandma was able to come home from the hospital. My Uncle Rob was waiting for my grandma and me to come home. Uncle Rob had dinner waiting for us.

After dinner, Grandma and I sat with Rob, and we all discussed what would happen. Grandma Betty suggested having Uncle Rob, me, and Grandma meet with my mom, Lily, at the park. So, I decided to call my mom and invite her to meet me at the park.

After about twenty minutes of talking to my mom, Lily, on the phone, I hung up and went back into the living room with my grandma and Uncle Rob. I then told them my mom would meet me at Valley Park tomorrow around noon. I then went to bed and got ready for the next day. It was going to be very hard and challenging to make my mom understand that Uncle Rob was still alive. he was going to be overwhelmed with mixed feelings.

It was morning time. I woke up, got ready, fixed my hair and makeup, and went to the kitchen for breakfast. Grandma Betty and Rob were waiting in the kitchen, ready to start the day.

Grandma looked at me and said, "Are you ready for today?"

I looked at her and shook my head, "No." I was apprehensive that Mom would not take this too well. "I mean, look at you. You had a heart attack when you found out Uncle Rob was alive."

Uncle Rob spoke up. He said, "Don't worry, everything will be okay," as he took a sip from his coffee cup.

We finished our breakfast and gathered in the driveway to get into the car and head to the park. Valley Park was about two hours from my grandma's house, so it was about an hour and a half away, maybe two hours away, from my mom's house. As we drove down the road, I was thinking of all the ways I could tell my mom that Uncle Rob was still alive. I just am so worried she won't take it too well. We listento country music, relax, and havea good old time in the car, just driving down the road at a normal speed, not hurrying to the park. But at the same time, I want to get this meeting with my mom over with.

I looked around, and I saw the park. We pulled up, and I saw my mom's car right next to the outbuilding.

I got out and said, "Uncle Rob, stay here until I wave you over."

I got out of the car. I wandered around the building, and there was my mom. She was waiting, swinging on a swing. She looked childlike and at ease. I almost didn't want to tell her that Uncle Rob was alive because she looked so comfortable and happy.

As I walked closer, she turned and glanced my way. She saw me, jumped off the swing, came running, and wrapped her arms around me.

I was so happy; I thought my mom was mad at me for everything I was doing. But she's forgiven me; I can do this. I have to be smart about it. I thought about it.

I asked my mom how she was doing, and we talked briefly for about fifteen minutes.

Then I decided I better tell her. So I said, "Mom, listen…"

She was all ears.

I blurted it out. I said, "Mom, Uncle Rob is alive."

My mom just stood there stunned, confused and in disbelief.

My mom started yelling at me, saying "I'm afraid that's wrong. What have you been drinking? I don't believe you. This is absurd."

I yelled back at my mom and asked her, "Why would I waste my time coming up here to tell you a lie or a story or make up this?"

My mom was about ready to leave.

I said, "Wait a second, I have proof. I will show you."

She stopped right in her tracks, turned around, and glared at me. She said, "This is a sick joke. What are you doing to me? What are you doing to your brothers? What are you doing to your family? These are lies."

Just as my mom said all this, I was waving my hands frantically, trying to get my Uncle Rob's attention.

My Uncle Rob saw me.

I was very frantic. I didn't know what to do; my mom yelled at me like I'd never had her yell at me. I was so confused and hurt that she would even think that I was making up such a lie.

My Uncle Rob came running over.

Just as I was ready to say, "Mom, he's alive," she turned around to see who was sneaking up behind her. She gasped for air, and she collapsed. She had fainted. Was she okay? What had I done? I bent over my mom, trying to wake her to get her to regain consciousness.

As I bent over my mom, her eyes opened, and my mom spoke and started muttering, "What? Your uncle's alive?"

I helped my mom up to her feet.

My mom looked into Rob's eyes. She started swearing at Uncle Rob. "Son of a bitch, how dare you?" My mom was yelling at Uncle Rob, saying, "How dare you? I thought you were dead." Suddenly, she grabbed Uncle Rob, wrapped her arms around him, and said, "I missed you so much."

My Uncle Rob and my mom decided to go to the other side of the park for privacy.

Grandma Betty and I decided to swing on the swing set, and my Uncle Rob and Mom got caught up. We finally decided it was time to head to Grandma's house. We said goodbye to my mom, and all three of us, Rob, Grandma, and I, took off in my car. We finally arrived at Grandma's house and we all got out of the car and headed into the house.

Grandma Betty said, "I'm going to cook dinner; you guys go wash up."

As Uncle Rob and I entered the living room, and sat down. I started asking him question after question. I was so curious about what Uncle Robin and Mom talked about. Uncle Rob finally sat down and told me that he had a home in Nevada and told my mom, Lily, to get the boys and come live with him in Nevada. Uncle Rob then looked at me and said I could go live with him too. I was so excited by this news, and after dinner, I wrote in my diary that I was so pleased with how the day turned out.

Early the next morning, I heard the doorbell ring, so I ran to the door, not knowing who to expect this early in the morning. As I opened the door, there were my mom and my three brothers. I grabbed my three brothers and gave them a big hug. I told them to come inside; they entered the living room and sat on the couch. My mom, Lily, sat on the chair next to the couch. I asked my mom if she told my brothers about Rob. As I asked my mom this, my brother Tony asked who Rob was. So, at this point, I knew my mom didn't say anything to my brothers yet.

My mom started explaining what was going to happen. She said that she and the boys would live with Rob in Nevada.

I told my mom that Uncle Rob said I could go live with him too.

My mom was so pleased to hear this. She said that she had packed their bags, and everything was in the car.

I asked her, "Are you guys leaving today?"

"She is leaving today with the boys," a voice came from nowhere. It was my Uncle Rob.

My Uncle Rob then turned to me and said. "Go pack your bags."

I ran to my room to pack my bags because I knew we had to leave before my dad, Fred, caught us. I packed my bags, then ran out to the living room, and said I was ready to go.

We all said goodbye to my Grandma Betty and went outside. Rob got in his car, my mom got in her own car with the boys, and then I loaded up in my car. We all followed each other in our own cars to head to Nevada and Uncle Rob's house.

As we drove, we soon arrived half a day later. We drove up this long driveway and found a ranch-style house with many farm animals. The different kinds of animals were chickens, goats, pigs, and horses. I knew I would love it here at Uncle Rob's. After we all unloaded our cars and put our bags and belongings away, my brothers, mom, and Uncle Rob met in the dining room for dinner. Everyone was so happy; they enjoyed their dinner and conversations. Uncle Rob started by welcoming us to his home. Then he asked my brothers and me what we liked about his farm.

Rick quickly answered, "I love the animals."

Then my other two brothers whispered, "We love the animals too."

I then spoke up, "I love the animals like everyone else."

Every day was like a new day with so many smells and scenery. There was so much to do on this ranch, and much needed fixing such as the fence of the barns and the chicken coop. I just wanted to feed all the animals, groom them, and help out this way. I was so excited when my mom said I could do homeschool. My mom wants my brothers to be homeschooled too.

About a year had passed, and finally, I was getting worried about my grandma; I hadn't heard from her for nearly a year. So I decided to go into the house and call her. The phone was ringing, and then I heard this quiet voice answer; it was my grandma.

I said, "Hi Grandma, how are you doing? What have you been up to?"

My grandma said quietly that she was not doing well. My dad, Fred, had been harassing her and trying to find out where I had gone and where my mom and brothers were. She's so scared she'll mess up and tell my dad everything.

All of a sudden, while I was talking to my Grandma Betty, I heard a voice on the other line. It was my dad, Fred.

He was upset he started yelling at Betty. hen he took the phone from her, and he started saying, "Who is this?"

I told Dad, "It's me."

He said, "Where are you?"

I told him, "I'm fine, and it's none of your business where I am."

My dad, Fred, started yelling at me," Do you know where your mom and your brothers are?"

I told Fred that my brothers and my mom were with me, and we were with Uncle Rob. "He's alive. He never died in that car accident."

Just as I yelled this information, I realized what I had done. My dad has a way of getting any information out of me. Every time someone yells at me, I have a habit of telling the person yelling at me anything to shut them up. This time, I went too far and told my dad too much.

Fred stopped yelling and all of a sudden, his voice changed. He sounded mean. He sounded evil.

He said, "I'm coming after you guys and getting you back."

I didn't know what to do, so I just hung up the phone; I was scared. I ran to tell my Uncle Rob and Mom what happened with my dad.

They were in the middle of cooking dinner in the kitchen when I rushed in, and they turned to me and asked me what was wrong. I blurted out that Fred knew everything.

My mom dropped her spatula and started screaming, "Does Fred know where we're at?"

I looked at her and said, "No, I don't think so, unless Grandma Betty tells him."

Uncle Rob then turned around, bent down, picked up the spatula, and told us not to worry.

A few weeks have passed, and no word from my grandma Betty. I almost feel like calling her and finding out if Fred is still looking for us or what Fred's plan is. That's it. I decided I would call my grandma.

It seemed to be ringing for a long time, but it was only ringing for a couple of seconds, and then my Grandma Betty answered. She was crying. I asked her what was wrong.

She said, "Fred found out where you guys live. He got a private investigator."

"Oh no," I said, "I got to go, Grandma."

I then hung up the phone, ran to my mom, and told her that Fred knows where we live.

My mom ran to the phone. She said, "We got to call your Uncle Rob. He's out getting fencing for the ranch."

Then the phone went dead and we heard somebody walking outside by the front door. I grabbed my momma's hand. A squeeze assured me that she was scared too.

I asked my mom, "Where are my brothers?"

She replied that they were over at a friend's house for the night. My brothers haven't wanted to be home since my mom told my brothers that Uncle Rob was their dad. They have been mad at my mom for a while now.

Suddenly, the front door creaked open, and I was squeezing my mom's hand by this time. Suddenly, we saw this hand, which had an axe in it. The body moved through the door, and to our wonder, it was Uncle Rob.

Suddenly, my mom yelled, "I felt scared, Rob."

My mom ran over to him and hugged him. My mom told Rob that Fred knew where they live. Uncle Rob threw down everything and started for the phone; he dialed 911 with shaky fingers. I could tell Uncle Rob was very scared; I could hear it in Uncle Rob's voice as he explained everything to the dispatcher on the phone. It was sunset by now, and Mom, Uncle Rob, and I gathered in the dining room with the meal that might be our last meal together as a family, I thought. I didn't know what my dad Fred had in store for Uncle Rob.

Suddenly, a car came driving up the road; we didn't recognize the car. Uncle Rob went to the front door to meet the person who drove up the driveway. It was a private detective. It was an old buddy of Uncle Rob's. I felt relieved. The man came in and sat down on the couch. He was all ears, listening attentively to what Uncle Rob had to say about my dad, Fred. The man said he would watch the ranch and call in the workforce. He knew that this was not good.

It was about time to get to bed, so my mom and I went to my room and talked. She was terrified, the same as me. I was terrified. I didn't know what to expect from my dad. Mom said goodnight, and I crawled into bed. I laid there turning and tossing all night. I was so distressed. After a long night of restlessness and no sleep, I woke slightly as my mom shook me awake. I was so exhausted, but I was scared at the same time.

I didn't realize what was happening, and my mom started screaming, "Get dressed, get dressed. He's here."

I said, "Who's here?"

Mom said, "Your father, Fred."

I jumped out of bed hurriedly and got dressed. At this time, I could hear some yelling going on in the living room. I finally got my pants, shoes, and shirt on. I ran into the living room and saw my dad, Fred, physically fighting with Rob. I started yelling at my dad, Fred, to calm down, but he wouldn't listen. He just kept on yelling.

Finally, I asked Mom where the workforce was last night, and my mom said that all the workforce was gone. They went for coffee and donuts this morning. They thought we would be okay, but Fred showed up an hour after they left. I yelled for my mom to go to the phone and call Uncle Rob's buddy, the private detective.

My mom yelled, "I don't have their number!"

Suddenly, I heard this crash, this bang, and then it went silent. There was no more yelling; I was so scared. I ran into the other room and saw Uncle Rob standing over my dad, Fred.

"What happened? Is my dad okay? I love my dad, and I don't want him to be hurt. I don't want him to hurt you either, Uncle Rob."

My Uncle Rob threw down the fire poker covered in blood. My Uncle Rob turned to my mother and said, "iIt's over. It is over. We can finally move on with our life."

I looked over at my dad. As I bent down, I felt for a pulse. I started crying. There was no pulse. My dad was gone. He was dead. I was so shocked; I just stared in disbelief.

I turned around and looked at my Uncle Rob with hatred. I ran to him. I started beating him with my fists. "How could you do this? How could you kill my dad? What were you thinking?"

My Uncle Rob held me in his arms so I couldn't pound on him anymore. He said, "Listen, I had no choice. One of us was going to die, and I didn't want it to be me."

I looked up at Uncle Rob; I understood now. "I'm sorry, Uncle Rob, I forgive you."

Just as I said this, a man walked into the room. He said everything was okay; it was a police officer. My Uncle Rob turned to him, explained what happened, and told him that he needed to call someone to pick up the body. A few hours passed, and my Uncle Rob went down to the station to report what happened at the house.

I said, "Mom, he sure has been gone a long time. I hope they don't put him in jail."

My mom gazed at me, took my hand, and said, "I love you. I don't know what's going to happen with your Uncle Rob."

My mom and I continued to chat, and finally, the phone rang. It was my Uncle Rob's caller ID. My mom answered the phone, took the phone call in the other room, and was on the phone for nearly an hour.

She returned and told me Uncle Rob said he'd be home shortly. I was relieved to find out that they wouldn't keep him overnight in the jail cell. I asked my mom when my brothers would be home; she said she had no idea but was hoping tomorrow.

My mom had dinner ready for Uncle Rob. When he showed up at the house, they sat down and started talking to me, telling me what the future would bring and their ideas of how we would live life. I was more worried for my brothers because they were so mad at my mom for not telling them Rob was their dad.

A few days passed, and there was no sign of my brothers. They were still at their friend's house. I was hoping to see them soon. I decided to call my grandma and tell her what had happened to my father because she had not heard yet, and I thought it was time to talk to her. As I was on the phone listening to it ring, I wondered how my grandma would handle this. She had a heart attack when she found out Rob was alive. What is she going to do when she finds out her son Fred is dead? That was a scary idea, but she needed to know the truth. All of a sudden, I heard her voice. She sounded so calm and happy. I didn't want to disturb her. I told her that my father Fred had found us and got into it with Uncle Rob. Uncle Rob killed Fred, and all of a sudden, the phone went silent. I was scared of what was happening. Did my grandma have another heart attack?

I said, "Grandma, Grandma, are you there? Are you okay?"

She then answered with a crackled voice, "Did you have a funeral for him?"

I didn't know how to answer her. I told her no, we did not; we had him cremated and no services. My grandma stated that she was disappointed in me for not having a funeral for my dad, Fred. I told her I was sorry and disappointed in myself, but I had no money, so we had to do it cheaply, putting it lightly.

My Grandma Betty started crying and said, "I have no one here. Can I come live with you guys? I don't want to live here alone anymore."

I told her I would talk to Uncle Rob and Mom and see what we could develop.

Later that night, when Mom and Uncle Rob were at the kitchen table, I brought up that Grandma wanted to come to live with us. Uncle Rob said yes, he would love for his mom to live with us. So, with that being said, the next day I headed to my grandma's. I was so excited it took me half a day, but when I reached my grandma's house, she was shocked and delighted to be able to finally come and live with Uncle Rob and us. I stayed at Grandma's for a few days before returning home with her to live with Uncle Rob and Mom; I was so happy that my grandma wanted to come live with us.

Days later, I was driving up the road to my Uncle Rob's house with my grandma.

"Everybody's going to be so excited to see you, Grandma."

As I pulled into the driveway, everyone was there waiting for my brothers, mom, and Uncle Rob; they were thrilled to see Grandma. We all went into the house and settled down for the night.

As the weeks went by, my mom became very secretive, and I wondered what this was all about; I wondered what secrets my mom was keeping besides the one about Uncle Rob being my brother's dad. My mom was acting so secretive that I was beginning to question every move she ever made and everything she ever said. My brothers were still angry at my mom for keeping such an important secret about the identity of their father. They had come home and rejoined the family sooner or later. I decided to make friends, so I started joining book clubs, baseball leagues, and gymnastics to have friends to hang out with finally.

A few months passed, and it was almost the new year. I was so excited that I had met so many good friends. I was looking forward to spending the day with my mom. By the way, it was my eighteenth birthday, and I was eager to start the day. We were going to have a great party for my eighteenth birthday. I finished school, graduated, and was ready to start life. It was finally time for the party. I was so relieved to see all my friends, my mom, Uncle Rob, my grandma, and my brothers at my birthday party. I had so much fun; I played many games like three-card poker, rummy, crazy eights, and solitaire; the party was great. All of my friends wanted to have a sleepover, stay the night, and play more games. My mom thought it was best for my friends to stay the night anyways after they had drank so much. The party seemed to last so long that I thought the day would never end; all my friends passed out later that night. It was just me and my mom, alone at last.

My mom took my hand in hers and said, "It's your eighteenth birthday, and I have to tell you something important, and I hope you're not going to hate me."

My mom took me by the hand and led me out the back door into the field. It was dark in the sky; the stars were shining in the sky so dim. The smell of cow manure took over the autumn air. I wondered what my mom had to say that she thought I would hate her. We walked down the row of corn out to the pond on the far side of the ranch. I looked at the water with the night sky reflecting off of black silk water. I gazed into my mom's eyes with a concerned look.

My mom then realized I was concerned and a little scared; she could see the fear in my eyes. My mom leaned in and hugged me. My mom said, "Everything is going to be alright, don't worry. I have to tell you something that could be the end of our relationship as mother and daughter."

As I listened to these words roll off her tongue, I became more worried about what she had to tell me. I was wondering what could be so bad that I would hate her.

My mom began with a story she said that she's not my birth mother; she's not my biological mother. She was stuttering as she somehow found the words to begin her story.

I was in disbelief; I couldn't believe it was this true.

My mom began with the story that she came into my life when I was six months old; she married Fred and became my mother. Fred is my biological father, but Lily is not my biological mother.

As Lily muttered these words, I was in disbelief, disappointed, and very angry. I was shocked, to say the least.

Lily continued with her story. "See, Lynn, your mother, your biological mother, was too young when she had you, and she was married to Fred, your father. She and your father had a disagreement, and your mother left Fred when you were six months old. She left you behind so she could go and have a life of her own. Fred didn't know where she went. Still, he knew he had to get you a mother, so Fred came and looked for me to replace your mother."

As I took every word in, it started to make sense why my mom was so different to me, why she was always keeping secrets from me and being secretive about everything, and how she always pulled away. It was all starting to make sense to me. Now, my whole life was unraveling before my eyes. I felt like I was going to lose it. I thought I was going to have a breakdown.

I didn't know what to say, so I pulled away from Lily. I blurted out, "You're not my birth mother, so that means my brothers aren't my brothers. They are my cousins. Oh my gosh…"

This has turned out to be the worst eighteenth birthday party; what do I do now? I had to find my mom, my biological mother. I backed away from Lily so far away that I fell into the water. I got up and was soaked from head to toe.

Lily just stood there in shock. I started to run towards the house. I didn't know what to do but knew I had to escape Lily. The first thing that came to mind was where my Uncle Rob was. I needed to talk to him. If anybody knew who my mom was, it would be my Uncle Rob. I ran to the house. I ran into the house.

I started yelling, "Uncle Rob, Uncle Rob, where are you?"

I heard a deep voice yelling from the family room. It was my Uncle Rob.

I ran in there and started crying. I could hardly talk. Uncle Rob asked what was wrong. I looked into his eyes, and I told him I found out Lily was not my biological mother; Rob just looked down. He was disappointed that I had found out the truth.

I looked up at him and said, "I need to know who my mother is; I need my mother. I don't have my father. He's dead because of you. I need my mother, my biological mother, not Lily."

My Uncle Rob took me in his arms and said, "Calm down; everything will be okay. I know who your mom is."

I said, "Who is my biological mother?"

He said, "No, I don't know who your biological mother is; I know your mother, and that's Lily."

I blurted out, "She's not my mother. Lily is not my mother."

Rob said, "I know Lily is not your biological mother, but she is your mother; she is the only mother you've ever known."

At this point, I pulled away from my Uncle Rob, threw my hands in the air, and said, "If you're not going to help me find my mother, my biological mother, I will have to find her myself. Do you at least know her name, Uncle Rob? Do you know my biological mother's name? You had to know who my dad, Fred, was married to at one time and was pregnant with me."

Just as this moment came, Lily burst in, yelling, "Rob, Rob, you won't believe what happened…"

My Uncle Rob then yelled back, "Lynn and I are in the family room."

Lily came in looking very distressed and upset; she said, "I'm so sorry, Rob, but I had to tell Lynn the truth."

Rob then grabbed my hand and said all, "I know is your mother's first name."

I looked at him with eagerness in my eyes to find out the truth at last.

Uncle Rob stated, "Her name was Sarah; that's all I know. I'm sorry I'm not much help."

I looked at my Uncle Rob and said, "Your friend that's the detective. Can he help me find out who my biological mother is?"

Rob looked at me, grabbed my hand even tighter, and said, "Of course I will talk to my friend; we will find out the truth together. I'll be here for you, Lynn, all the way."

I looked at Lily and Rob and started crying. They both took me into their arms and shared a hug with me. I felt relieved but worried about telling my brothers they were my cousins, not my biological ones.

At this moment, I asked Uncle Rob and Lily what we should do about Tony, Jimmy, and Ricky.

Lily then spoke. She said, "What about them? What do they need to know? We could keep this a secret from them. They don't ever have to know."

I was stunned. "How could we keep this a secret? I can't go on believing that they're my brothers when they're not. They have to know the truth, Lily and Uncle Rob."

Lily then spoke. "I believe that that would be the best."

At this time, I heard my brothers coming down the hall; they walked into the family room, looked at us, and asked what was happening. I burst into tears and ran over to them. I gave all three of them a hug at the same time, and I told them they had to sit down. I then spoke openly with my brothers, who are my cousins, and I told them the whole story, everything that Lily told me once again.

They were mad at their mother, Lily, for keeping so many secrets, and they were sad for me. They reached out their hand and said, "You'll always be our sister and will always love you as our sister and nothing else."

I grabbed their hands and told them, "I love you guys; you are the best."

www.ingramcontent.com/pod-product-compliance
Lightning Source LLC
Chambersburg PA
CBHW072143150726
48002CB00004B/1611